By Bill Peet

BIG BAD BRUCE

Houghton Mifflin Company Boston

Library of Congress Cataloging in Publication Data

Peet, Bill.
  Big bad Bruce.

  SUMMARY: Bruce, a bear bully, never picks on
anyone his own size until he is diminished in more
ways than one by a small but very independent
witch.
  [1. Bears--Fiction. 2. Witches--Fiction]
I. Title.
PZ7.P353Bi   [E]   76-62502
ISBN 0-395-25150-8

Printed in the United States of America

ISBN 0-395-25150-8 Reinforced Edition
ISBN 0-395-32922-1 Sandpiper Paperbound Edition
WOZ   30 29 28 27

Forevergreen Forest was a quiet peaceful place until Bruce, a great shaggy brute of a bear came wandering up out of a canyon one day. A bear of such size was enough to frighten anyone, and the smaller creatures who lived there kept a sharp eye on Bruce in case he might give them trouble.

As long as Bruce was busy rooting around under boulders and logs searching for a feast of beetles and grubs there was no need to worry.

But when the big fellow was feeling frisky and ready for fun it was time to beware of the bear. What Bruce called fun was to scare the wits out of everyone.

The most fun of all for Bruce was rock tumbling. There were
lots of rocks in Forevergreen Forest — great jumbles of them. With
a swipe of a paw the bear sent them tumbling down the steep slopes

4

three and four at a time. The tumbling rocks shattered logs and flattened the bushes and brush, leaving no place for the rabbits and quail to hide. So they took off in a panic to go leaping and dodging and flying pell-mell in every direction.

Once he had them all on the run, Bruce went rolling around on the ground exploding into great roaring snorting fits of laughter, "Haw! Haw! Har! Har! Haw! Haw! Ho! Ho!"

As long as the bear lived in Forevergreen Forest it would never be peaceful and quiet again, and for all anyone could see he had come there to stay.

Then one afternoon Bruce made an awful mistake, a terrible blunder. He came across a huge boulder resting on a bluff and decided to give it a ride.

With a mighty heave he sent the boulder tumbling down a steep slope "Flumpity! Blumpity Whumpity Whump!," smashing pine trees and aspens to splinters and leaving deep dents in the ground as it went.

In one last big bounce it landed "Kerplump!" in a berry patch, just missing an old woman and her cat by a whisker. It was Roxy, a crafty little witch who was out picking blueberries with her cat Klinker.

"Where in blazes did you come from?!!" she shrieked, giving the boulder a vicious kick. "How did you get here?! Who sent you?!"

Just then a raucous roar of laughter echoed through the pines, and in a twinkle Roxy caught sight of the bear on the bluff. "So that's who!" she cried. And in a fury she went storming up the slope to face the bear.

"You big lummox!" she exploded. "You big bumbling brute! That rock could have squashed us to smithereens! And you think it's funny!"

"Har! Har!" chortled Bruce. "Ho! Ho! Hee! Hee! Har! Har!"
The bear had never seen anything half so funny as the frantic little woman with the wild flying hair.

"Laugh while you can," warned the witch, "but just wait. I'll have the last laugh, Mister Bear. Oh, indeed I will!"

Then she took off like a shot, to go streaking down the slope so fast her cat could barely keep pace. And when the witch reached her cabin at the edge of the forest she had hatched a plot.

"I'll make a pie," she decided. "A very special pie for ole Mister Bear."

In a flicker of an eye she made the pie crust, and in a trizzle and a trice she whipped up a filling of blueberries and honey.

"Now for the trickery," she muttered, flipping through her magical cookbook to one of her favorite recipes. Then, reading the directions carefully, Roxy began to measure. "One drop of dwindling. Two blurps of belittling. A smidgeon of minikin. A half teaspoon of twurp. A shrift of shortening. And then one pinch of kapoot should do it!"

The instant the pie was baked a golden brown and ready to serve
Roxy scurried out the door with it, back to the forest. Then, keeping
an eye out for the bear, she crept along through the shadows as
slinky as a fox.

When she reached a small clearing near the spot where she had
met the bear there was not a sign of him. But she could hear him
snorting and snooting around in the brush somewhere up the slope.
Quickly she picked out a pine stump, jerked off her apron and flung
it over the top, then put the pie on it.

"The table's all set," she whispered. "Now skit-scat! Kittycat!
Let's get lost!" And they ducked down behind a log just a hop skip
and a jump from the stump to wait for ole Mister Bear.

They didn't wait long. Pretty soon a whiffle of breeze sent the sweet aroma of blueberries and honey drifting up to Bruce and he followed his snuffling nose straight to the stump, snatched up the pie in his paws, and in one "Chomp!" and a "Slurp!" it was gone.

"Ho! Ho!" cackled Roxy, popping up from behind the log, "I tricked you, Mister Bear! Ho! Ho! *Did I ever!*"

Bruce didn't like being surprised and he let go with an angry "Grrrowf!"

"Grrrowf yourself!" Roxy shot back. "You don't scare me. Just watch out you don't get pecked to bits by a quail, or stomped on by a rabbit."

"Snurf!" snorted the grumpy bear, and he wheeled around and lumbered off into the underbrush.

Bruce hadn't gone very far when he began feeling drowsy — so drowsy he could hardly keep his eyes open — so he flopped down against a tree trunk to rest, and in the time it takes for one big yawn, he dropped off to sleep.

While the bear slept he gradually began to grow smaller. Inch by inch and little by little Bruce dwindled away. He kept shrinking and shriveling until he was down to the size of a possum. And still he kept shrinking. When the diminishing spell was finally finished the bear had dwindled all the way down to the size of a chipmunk.

Bruce was awakened by a sharp peck on the head, and with an angry growl that came out like a squeak he reared up all ready to fight.

But when he found himself nose to beak with a giant of a quail Bruce backed off to gape in amazement. Then as the bewildered bear looked around he was surprised by three more giant quail and a pair of huge rabbits.

The rabbits and quail had recognized Bruce and as they closed
in to attack he quickly turned tail and went plowing headlong into
a tangle of brambles. But there was no chance of outrunning the
rabbits and quail in a thicket. They were close on his heels, pecking
and stomping the bear with a fury.

Bruce didn't dare try to fight back. He kept ducking and dodging his way through the brambles, frantically searching for someplace to hide — a gopher hole, a flat rock to squeeze under, any place at all.

At last he stumbled into a forest of cattails at the edge of a creek and in a flying leap flung himself into the water — "Ker-sploosh!" — and bobbed up well beyond reach of the rabbits and quail.

Then, kicking and thrashing with all four feet Bruce headed for the opposite bank, which was a long long swim for a tiny bear. About halfway across a sudden swirl of current sent him spinning around and around, upside down and under.

Bruce was about to be swept down the twisting creek and away
forever when he grabbed onto a rock and managed to haul himself
out of the water.

Then the bruised and bedraggled bear sprawled out on his belly
choking and wheezing and snorting out bubbles until at last he was
able to breathe.

For a long time he lay there staring into the swirling stream, trying to figure out what could have happened to make him so small.

He wondered if it might have been something he ate. Suddenly he remembered the blueberry pie and the fierce little woman who had warned him: "Watch out you don't get pecked to bits by a quail, or stomped on by a rabbit!" All at once Bruce realized he had been tricked by a crafty old witch! *Shrunk* by a magic spell!

By this time the sun had gone down and deep shadows had crept across the creek. A chilly breeze rippled the dark water and the soggy wet bear shivered and shook from the cold and also from fright. Bruce knew that the night hunters were already out on the prowl, and now he was fair game. The jittery bear sat up on his haunches looking all about in the dark for any sign of danger. He looked everywhere but up, or he would have seen the frowsy old owl peering down from a tree limb above. The fuzzy little brown thing on the rock was a choice tidbit for the owl and he was just about to swoop down when all of a sudden —

— a screechy voice split the air. "Mister Bear! Mister Bear!" With a terrified "HOOT," the owl sailed off into the night, leaving the bear to face another kind of danger.

In desperation Bruce scrunched himself up into a ball, hoping the witch would mistake him for part of the rock. But there was no chance of fooling foxy old Roxy, and holding her lantern out over the creek she spotted the bear in a flash.

"Ho! Ho!" she cackled. "There you are, Mister Bear! No bigger than a minute! Quick! Quick! Klinker! Go fetch him! Skit! Scat!"

Before the bear could blink an eye the cat snatched him off the rock by the scruff of the neck and leaped lightly back to the bank.

"Good cat!" cried Roxy. "Now home we go! But easy does it! This little bear has had a big day."

As Bruce was carried along through the dark forest he didn't dare put up a struggle. Besides, he was too weary to even lift a paw — and much too scared.

He was sure the crafty old witch planned to fix him for good. If she could shrink him down to a runt of a thing she could turn him into a tadpole, or into a flea, or make him disappear altogether.

But to the bear's surprise the witch turned out to be a kindly old woman and as gentle as could be, just as long as she kept her temper. Roxy loved flowers and birds and animals, especially small animals. And she soon grew very fond of the tiny bear, so she decided to keep him that way.

Klinker the cat also took a liking to the bear and they ate out of the very same bowl and slept in the same corner together under the kitchen stove.

Little bears have short memories and in a few days Bruce forgot all about ever being a giant of a bear. For all he knew Roxy's flower garden was a beautiful leafy green forest with plenty of room to roam. Whenever the tiny bear was feeling frisky and ready for fun he flipped pebbles around as if they were boulders just to scare the wits out of the grasshoppers, the beetles and caterpillars. From a bug's-eye view Bruce was a great big hairy-scary horrible brute of a beast.

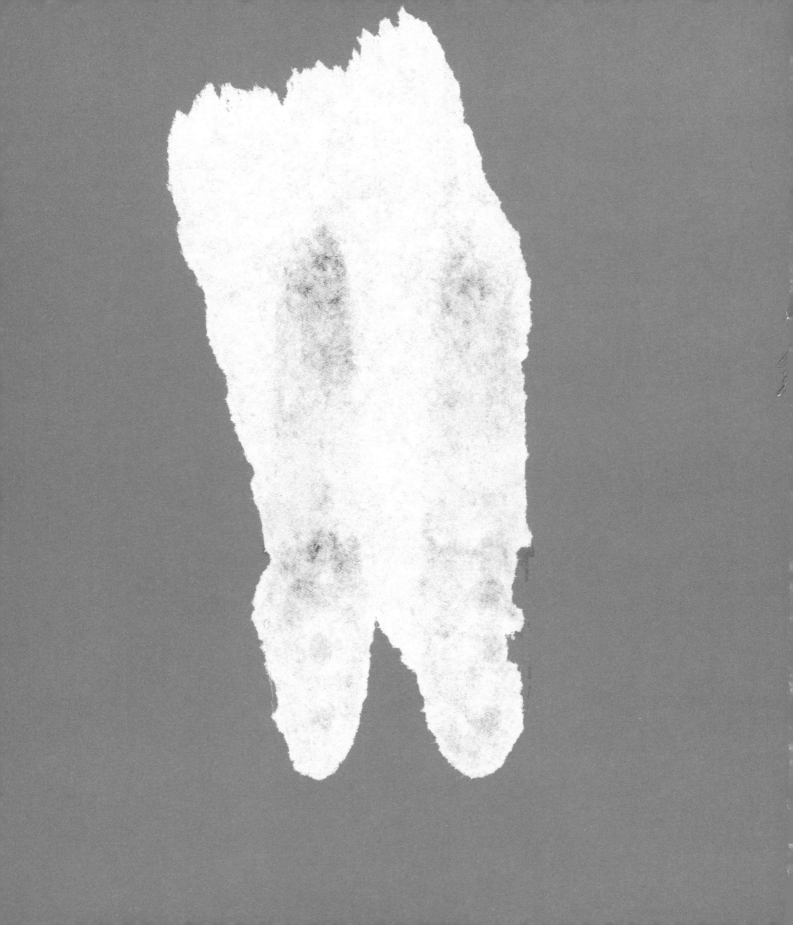